FORCED OUT

FORCED OUT

Gene *Fehler*

MINNEAPOLIS

Darby Creek
A division of Lerner Publishing Group, Inc.
241 First Avenue North
Minneapolis, MN 55401 U.S.A.

Website address: www.lernerbooks.com

The images in this book are used with the permission of: © Kelpfish/Dreamstime.com, p. 117; © iStockphoto.com/Jill Fromer, p. 120 (banner background); © iStockphoto.com/Naphtalina, pp. 120, 121, 122 (brickwall background). Front Cover: © Getty Images/Taxi/Getty Images. Back Cover: © Kelpfish/Dreamstime.com.

Main body text set in Janson Text 12/17.5.
Typeface provided by Adobe Systems.

Fehler, Gene, 1940–
Forced out / Gene Fehler.
p. cm. — (Travel team)
ISBN: 978–0–7613–8321–5 (lib. bdg. : alk. paper)
[1. Baseball—Fiction.] I. Title.
PZ7.F3318Fo 2012
[Fic]—dc23 2011027145

Manufactured in the United States of America
1—BP—12/31/11

To Mirielle, Gabrielle,
and Kayla

“The way a team plays as a whole determines its success. You may have the greatest bunch of individual stars in the world, but if they don't play together, the club won't be worth a dime.”

—BABE RUTH

CHAPTER 1

Second baseman Zack Waddell kept up his nonstop chatter. One more out and the Roadrunners would extend their winning streak to eleven games. The only problem: the San Antonio Aztecs had the tying run on third and the lead run on first.

Zack's Las Vegas–based travel team was ranked ninth nationally. They wanted to keep that ranking.

While closer Travis Melko stood just off

the pitcher's mound taking a couple deep of breaths, Zack glanced around at his outfield. He motioned for right fielder Sammy Perez to move a couple steps closer to the foul line. Even though the Aztecs' little left fielder, Paco, batted right-handed, Zack knew he liked to punch the ball to right. The best way to play him was to pitch him hard and inside, but to play him almost like a left-handed pull hitter. If he did try to hit to left he'd most likely get the ball in on his fists and pop it up or hit a weak grounder.

Even though this was Zack's first season with the Roadrunners, the reason head coach Scott Harris had recruited him from a local Las Vegas high school team to play for this elite seventeen-and-under travel team was because he was like a second coach on the field. Though Zack didn't actually play the real game of chess, people who watched him knew that the diamond was like his chessboard. He always knew how and when each piece should move.

Unfortunately, Melko didn't pitch Paco high and tight like he was supposed to.

Instead, he got the pitch on the outside half of the plate, and Paco drove it over first baseman Gus Toomey's head. The ball dropped just inside the foul line. Sammy's desperate dive came up inches short, and the ball skipped past him to the wall. Sammy bounced up and chased it down. He made a perfect throw to Zack for the relay home. Zack then took the throw and spun. But the lead run was already crossing the plate. Gus, the cutoff man, shouted "three!" while pointing toward third. Zack rifled the ball toward third, and shortstop Carlos "Trip" Costas cut off his throw, holding Paco at second. Trip called time and walked the ball to Melko.

Travis slammed the ball into his mitt. Zack shook his head. *You can't pitch Paco outside*, he said to himself. But he dared not say it out loud. He knew well enough that even the best big-league pitchers couldn't hit their spot all the time. It wasn't fair to blame Melko.

What was done was done, but now the Roadrunners were in real trouble. Down one run was bad enough. Being two runs down to the Aztecs' closer, Smithson, would make it tough. He was as hard a thrower as they had faced all season. He'd come in with two outs on in the eighth and shut down the Runners. It would be hard to score even one against him.

But Zack had a special trick up his sleeve—a play designed just for this situation.

Now was the perfect time to use it.

CHAPTER 2

In a typical pickoff play Zack would signal the catcher. The catcher would then flash the signal. The pitcher and shortstop would count to three. And at three, the ball and the infielder should both be at second base, ideally a split second before the runner got back there.

Zack had added an extra touch, though. The pitchers and Zack and Trip had worked a lot on this particular variation. At the count of one, Trip would break for second. The runner would head back with him. At the count of two, Trip would break back to his shortstop position. The runner might relax for a split second and come back off the bag. At the count of three, Zack and the ball would both be there. Sometimes the movement of the shortstop would fake out the runner. The play didn't work all the time, of course, but it worked often enough, especially if the Roadrunners hadn't already used it on their opponent. That's why they sometimes went several games without running the play. They only used it when the game was on the line.

Zack signaled catcher Nick Cosimo. Nick flashed the sign to Travis and Trip. At the count of three, Zack was at second base, taking the throw from Travis. A surprised Paco frantically threw himself headfirst back toward the bag. Zack slapped his glove on Paco's hand just before it got to the base. The ump got the call right. The Roadrunners sprinted toward the dugout, whooping it up all the way.

They didn't let up once they got to the dugout, either. The bad news: the top of the Roadrunners' batting order had hit in the eighth inning. They'd have the fifth, sixth, and seventh batters coming up. Still, there was really no weak spot in the lineup.

Assistant Coach Bobby Washington, or Wash, as he was better known, quieted the dugout.

"Sit on his fastball," he said. "He's not going to let himself get beat by throwing his second-best pitch. If he gets two strikes on you, he might throw his curve as a wasted pitch. Be aware of it. But be looking first for the heater."

Trip led off. Wash was right. Trip got six straight fastballs. Two were high. Trip swung at the other four. He got just a piece of each, fouling them off. With the count 2–2, Trip watched the curve drop low and outside. The count went full. Trip sat on the next fastball, which was around his shoulders. He knew he couldn't catch up with it, so he stopped his swing. He knew it was ball four. The ump agreed, and Trip trotted down to first base.

Danny Manuel, the Roadrunners' center fielder, saw nothing but fastballs. The third was right where he liked it, and he drove it to the gap in left center for a double. Coaching at third, Wash gave Trip the stop sign. A play at the plate would have been close. With nobody out, sending him home would have been too big a gamble.

Zack was up. A base hit would almost certainly score Trip from third and Danny from second, who represented the winning run. But Zack didn't even entertain the thought that he could be the hero by driving in the two most important runs.

A base hit would be a good bonus. But Zack knew his job was just to bring the tying run home and make sure Danny got to third base. A bunt was a possibility, but it was risky. Zack glanced at Wash from the third base coaching box. He wasn't surprised when he didn't see the bunt sign.

The Aztec infield played halfway, so that a hard-hit ball right at someone could keep the tying run from scoring. If they instead played in, any kind of ground ball could get through and two runs would score. And if they played deep, they'd be almost conceding the tying run.

Zack was patient at the plate. On the first pitch he took a strike on the inside corner. The next pitch was high for ball one. The Aztecs were obviously wary of the bunt, as a high, hard fastball is a hard pitch to bunt. The third pitch was high too. But it was on the outside part of the plate, right where Zack liked it. He swung and thought for a second he might have the game-winning hit, but his grounder between first and second was run down by the second baseman.

After he was thrown out at first, Zack jogged back to the dugout to accept high fives. Although his hit hadn't won his team the game, it had allowed Trip to score the tying run. And Danny was now on third, ninety feet away from giving the Roadrunners the championship.

The game was up to Nick now, the number-eight hitter in the lineup. The thing was, though, that Nick wasn't a typical number-eight hitter. He was good enough to bat cleanup for a lot of teams. The Aztecs knew this, so they walked him intentionally to set up the double play and face the pitcher, Travis.

But Travis didn't bat.

Ricky Mixon, a utility infielder who didn't see a lot of playing time, was sent up to pinch-hit. And the Aztecs probably didn't know that Ricky was the team's best bunter, better even than Zack.

The Roadrunners fans knew. Most of them in the bleachers were probably nudging each other and saying, "Second pitch, second pitch."

And it was. Ricky took a first-pitch strike. On the second pitch, the Roadrunners tried a suicide squeeze. Smithson saw it in time to throw the pitch inside, but Ricky still managed to get the ball down.

Danny was across home plate just as Smithson bent for the ball, saw it was hopeless, and gave it a hard kick across the third baseline. It barely missed Coach Harris, who had already come out from the dugout to congratulate his players.

Zack knew the reason why the Roadrunners kept winning was that they were a team of not just one hero, but many. Not many teams could count on a utility player to drive in the winning run in a big game. The Runners had what baseball people like to call "team chemistry."

CHAPTER 3

After the locker-room celebration, Coach Harris said, "A well-played tournament. You did yourselves proud. Consider those games a fine meal. Now I hope you're ready for dessert." The silver-haired head coach, who was fifty-six years old but more fit than most men twenty years younger, smiled broadly.

Zack nudged Nick and whispered, "Dessert? What's that supposed to mean?"

Coach Harris glanced his way and grinned. "You remember Wash and me telling you we didn't have room in our budget to enter the week-long, ninety-six-team tournament in New York later this summer?" He paused for a moment. "Well, I'm glad to tell you that has changed. We *will* be going to that tournament."

The room burst into cheers.

Coach Harris raised his hand to restore quiet.

"I want you to know right now how valuable this tournament will be. Not just for the team and for our chance to show that we can compete against the best U17 teams in the country, but for each of you individually. Each of you has talent. In New York, you'll have a chance to display that talent."

As they left the locker room, Zack and Nick were practically hyperventilating, they were so excited.

"Do you know how big this is?" Nick said. "There'll be major-league scouts and college representatives there. This is our big chance to show them what we can do."

"Especially if we can take the championship," Zack agreed. "Prove to all those scouts that we're a team of winners. I wonder how Coach pulled this one off!"

"That's a good question," Nick mused.

Zack grinned. "Maybe somebody won the lottery."

It wasn't Zack's concern where the money had come from. All that mattered was that he'd be playing baseball in New York before tons of scouts.

He knew he wasn't dreaming, but he pinched himself anyway.

Just to make sure.

. . .

Zack's mother was waiting for him in the parking lot. Zack was more amused than ashamed that his mother's car was one of the oldest models driven by any Roadrunners player or parent. Zack usually got a ride with one of the guys. Gus and Carson Jamison both had really fancy cars. But Zack knew his mother liked picking him up. So he let her do it once in a while.

Zack's dad had died two years earlier. Unfortunately, he hadn't left much money behind. That was why Zack and his mother were now living in an apartment, after moving out of their nice three-bedroom house.

What Zack's dad did leave behind, however, was everything he had taught Zack about baseball. At least Zack had that. At the start of almost every game he remembered to say to himself, *I'll try to make you proud, Dad.*

"That was an exciting game!" Zack's mom yelled through the open car window as he approached the car. "That pickoff play was terrific. I noticed that the boy avoided making eye contact with his coach all the way back to their dugout."

"I'm glad it worked," Zack said. "They're a tough team. We missed on a couple scoring chances early. It almost cost us."

"It didn't in the end, though. The Runners can always find a way to win. I'm so glad you get to play on a team like this."

"Well, it costs a lot of money," Zack said, opening the door of his mom's rusted-out minivan. "Even with the team taking care of most of the cost for me."

"We get by." Zack's mom smiled at him as she backed out of the parking spot. "You know we could never pass up this opportunity."

"Speaking of opportunities," Zack said. And he told her about the New York tournament.

"Be careful, Mom!" Zack said. She was so excited she almost ran a red light.

"Sorry!" she gasped.

Zack knew his mother's dream for him, largely because it had been his father's dream for him, was for Zack to become a big-league player. It was Zack's dream too, but he knew the chances were slim. Of the Roadrunners' seven other starters, not counting pitchers, five hit for a higher average and five hit for more power. He had only slightly better than average running speed.

Still, Zack was considered a winner. Every team he had ever played on was a winner. And while he lacked the physical skills of some of the other players, no one was a greater student of the game. His baseball instincts were as good as anyone's. But as for his dream, and his mother's, of him making the pros—Zack feared that's all it was, a dream. Good baseball instincts could take a player only so far.

Still, pro ball was a good dream. Zack had decided a long time ago to let his mother hold on to it.

CHAPTER 4

Zack understood how tight money was for his family. That's why he was so surprised when, just after joining the Roadrunners, one of the first things his mother said was, "You need your own bat."

On his high school team, Zack had always used one of the team bats. On the Roadrunners, however, almost all the players had their own personal, and expensive, bats. Zack told his mom he could get along without his own bat. The team had bats he could use.

But she wouldn't hear of it. "It makes a big difference, having just the right bat," she said. "We both know it."

So Zack's mother made sure he got a bat. And Zack's bat was so special, so crucial to his success, that he'd even named it.

Solomon.

Zack loved that bat. It represented his new team—the Roadrunners. He had never thought he'd have his own bat, much less an opportunity to play on a team like the Runners.

But all that had changed a few weeks earlier when he heard that surprising message on his voice mail.

"I'm calling for Zack Waddell," the voice had said. "This is Scott Harris. I'm coach of the Las Vegas Roadrunners." He had asked Zack to call him and had left a number.

Even then, Zack already knew who the Roadrunners were. Only one of the best U17 travel teams in the country.

Zack could think of only one reason why Coach Harris might want to talk to him. He was probably calling to get a scouting report about some high school player against whom Zack had played.

Zack returned the call. He was surprised to find out that Coach Harris was actually interested in seeing *him*.

. . .

The day Coach Harris came over to meet Zack and his mother, Zack was a nervous wreck. He couldn't understand why Harris thought *he* was Roadrunners material. Zack was sure it was all just a big mistake, and Harris would be embarrassed when he realized he'd contacted the wrong player.

"Hello, Mrs. Waddell," he said as he entered their small apartment. "I'm Scott Harris. My players call me Coach."

Zack's mom led him to the living room. The three of them sat. Zack could barely look at Harris. This couldn't be happening.

But Coach Harris turned to Zack. "Zack, I'd love to have you play for the Roadrunners. I've seen you play several times this spring. You'd be a big asset to our team."

"Oh wow," Mrs. Waddell said. Zack saw the look of surprise on her face. He knew his mother hadn't expected this any more than he had. Zack couldn't make his mouth form words.

The Runners' lineup last year had been full of .400 hitters and guys who could hit the long ball. On his high school team that spring, as a sophomore, Zack was his team's third-best hitter at .383. He'd hit two home runs. In his eight-team conference, Zack had played against several guys who hit better than he did.

There were more than sixty public and private high schools in the Las Vegas area. How had Coach Harris even been able to see him play enough to want him on the Roadrunners? And out of what were probably at least a thousand players from those teams, why him?

Zack knew he could play second base better than most anybody he'd played against. But the Roadrunners, that was a whole new ballgame. They were a team of all-stars, the best high school players from the best teams.

But Harris really did want him. It wasn't a joke.

Suddenly, Zack felt like he was soaring, his head above the clouds.

Then his mother asked the question that brought him crashing down: "How much would it cost for Zack to be on your team?"

Coach Harris explained the fees, and Zack watched in horror was his mother's face fell. He knew she could never afford this.

Some expenses were expected. Zack knew, of course, that he'd be responsible for his own equipment. He hadn't realized that the Roadrunners had to purchase their uniforms, though. Parents were responsible for travel expenses if they drove to games and stayed over in a hotel. They were responsible for food. Various tournaments had registration fees. There were umpire and field fees as well, and often players were expected to share those expenses.

"I'd love for Zack to play," Zack's mom said with a sigh. "But there's no way we can come up with that kind of money."

"The good news," Coach Harris said, "is that we have sponsors who pay a large part of the expenses. Even better news is that we always leave room on our roster for two scholarship players. These are players whose families' financial situations would not otherwise permit them to play for the Roadrunners."

"So exactly how much expense are we talking about for Zack to play with the Roadrunners?"

Coach Harris told her.

Zack looked at his mother, hopeful.

She smiled. "I think we can manage that."

It was all Zack could do to keep from jumping up and shouting.

He had been chosen to play for the Roadrunners. He would do everything possible to make sure Coach Harris didn't regret it.

CHAPTER 5

Now, several weeks into the season, Zack knew he hadn't let down Coach Harris. At least, not yet.

The team had a day off after their big win over the Aztecs, but the next day they were back at it with a 6:00 P.M. workout. At 5:30, Zack was watching for Nick's car and was outside even before Nick drove up to the apartments.

Zack ran up to the car, tossed his bag in the backseat and jumped in front. If Zack couldn't use his mother's car, Nick was able to pick him up most of the other times.

"It's not out of my way," Nick had said.

Nick was the same height as Zack, but he was about thirty pounds heavier. He wasn't fat, just stocky. He provided a good target for the Roadrunners' pitchers. He was durable too. He was built to withstand some hard slides at home plate. The few runners who had tried to barrel over Nick usually got the worst of it.

Nick was strong, and he could hit, handle pitchers, and throw. Maybe the only thing that could keep him out of the big leagues someday was his slower-than-average running speed. But there had been plenty of big-league catchers who couldn't run well.

Well, one other thing could keep him out too, Zack supposed. The fact that Nick had told them he was gay didn't matter to Zack or to the other Roadrunners. But Zack didn't know of any gay players in big-league baseball, at least none who had admitted it. Zack hoped something like that wouldn't keep Nick out of the pros, though.

"You hear the big news?" Nick said as they got on the road.

"What news?"

"We've got a new guy on our team."

"I thought our roster was set."

"So did everybody. But Trip heard about it from Nellie. I don't know who told him. I guess it's true, though." Nellie Carville was the team's captain. He wasn't one to spread rumors.

Nick glanced toward Zack and continued, "Here's the thing. He's come on to play second base. I guess Coach thinks we need more batting punch from the seven spot in the order."

Zack's shock must have shown on his face. Nick chuckled. "I'm kidding, man. You know your spot's safe. We need you on the field all the time."

"What position *does* he play?"

Nick paused for a second before answering. "Catcher."

Zack laughed. "No. Really."

Nick shrugged. "I'm serious. Trip told Nellie the guy's a catcher. From some private high school."

"Why would Coach bring in a catcher? We've got a good backup in Kevin in case you get hurt."

"Hey, don't even think that. That's a jinx, talking about a guy getting hurt. Like mentioning a no-hitter in the dugout."

"I don't believe in that stuff," Zack said.

"Not superstitious?" Nick raised his eyebrows. "Then why do you always mutter 'Okay, Solomon' when you get in the on-deck circle?"

"I didn't think anybody could hear that. I'm just saying it to myself."

"Oh, we hear it. But if it works, hey, good for you."

"So what's this catcher going to do?" Zack asked. "Be a cheerleader? He's not going to get any playing time. He must play at least one other position."

"I guess we'll find out today. Nellie said the guy is supposed to be at practice."

"Maybe he'll be so good you'll have to move to another position. Center field, maybe?"

Even Nick had to smile at Zack's joke—the thought of someone with his lack of speed trying to play center field. "Nice one," he said.

CHAPTER 6

Zack recognized the new player right away. It took him only a few seconds to place where he'd seen him.

It had been just this past spring, early in his high school's spring season. They had played a non-conference at Pearson Hill Academy, a private school about forty miles from Las Vegas. As soon as their team bus had driven through the gates, everyone suddenly grew silent.

Outside of a major-league stadium it was the most magnificent ballpark Zack had ever seen. A huge sign at the park's entrance read "Conover Stadium." It was pretty groomed, with big, bright lights. The seats even looked comfortable. Zack had never seen a ballpark this fancy at a high school.

After the seeing the outstanding ballpark, the game itself was almost anticlimatic. Pearson Hill was no match for Zack's team. The score of 13–5 was closer than the game itself. Zack's coach played three second-stringers most of the game and put a freshman hurler on the mound for the final two innings.

Nobody talked much about the game on the bus ride home. All they could talk about were the different buildings on campus, the landscaping, and of course, the athletic fields. It had been like traveling in another world.

"You must have to be a millionaire to be able to send your kid there," someone said.

No one challenged the statement.

• • •

The moment Zack saw the Roadrunners' new player he recognized him as Pearson Hill's catcher. Zack had played against him only that one time. And nothing stood out about the guy in Zack's memory. No powerful hitting or great defensive plays. But nothing bad, either. Zack's team had stolen a couple bases early without being thrown out. Then the coach shut down the running game, not wanting to run up the score. Zack didn't remember what kind of arm the catcher had.

Now, with this kid from Pearson Hill at his side, Coach Harris quieted the locker room.

"I'd like to introduce our newest player," he said. "This is Dustin Conover. Make him feel welcome."

Conover.

Zack knew exactly where he'd seen that name before.

• • •

Zack had just reached the edge of the infield when Dustin Conover walked over to him.

"I know you," Dustin said, grinning. "You played second base against us this spring. Pearson Hill Academy. You whipped us good. Not one of our better games. I remember you bunting one toward third. It sat down halfway down the line, two inches fair. We were all trying to wish it foul. One heck of a bunt."

"Thanks, man. Your name's Conover. Conover Stadium?"

Dustin shrugged. "What can I say? My dad doesn't go halfway on things."

"They named it after him?"

"He paid for it." Dustin paused for a few seconds before saying, "We moved out here from New York when I was in fourth grade. I've been at the Academy ever since. After I'd been there a few years, my dad decided the school needed a new stadium and practice fields."

"Hey Zack!"

Zack turned. Trip held a ball in the air. When he saw he had Zack's attention he tossed it to him.

"Later," Zack said to Dustin. He tossed the ball back to Trip. As they loosened up,

Zack's mind kept trying to get around what Dustin had just told him. How expensive were those things that Mr. Conover had bought for Pearson Hill? Zack thought about his baseball bat and how being able to afford one had seemed almost an impossibility.

Dustin's father had paid for a *whole stadium*. And more.

Zack glanced over at Dustin, who was playing catch with Kurt Kinnard, one of the Roadrunners' pitchers. Just looking at Dustin, you wouldn't think of him as a millionaire's kid, which was obviously what he was. He just looked like a ballplayer. A little over six feet tall, maybe 190. Watching him throw, Zack didn't see anything that made him think Dustin didn't belong on the Roadrunners.

Many of the Roadrunners came from wealthy families. Some, like Carson and Trip, had parents who were big sponsors of the team. They had more money than Zack knew he'd ever see, unless, of course, he made the big leagues some day. But that was about as likely as sixty inches of snow falling on Las Vegas in July.

Not even in his wildest dreams could he imagine himself pulling down one of those hundred-million-dollar contracts some players were getting for five or six years of playing ball. Even a year or two in the big leagues should be enough to set up a guy for life.

Zack wondered what had brought Dustin to the Roadrunners. Dustin obviously didn't have to dream of going far enough in baseball to earn the big money. From what Zack could tell, he already had it.

Zack also wondered if Dustin really had what it took to help the Roadrunners. And whether he was actually good enough to challenge Nick for the starting spot behind the plate. Zack hoped not.

• • •

Dustin didn't do anything outstanding in practice. In infield drills, he seemed to have a decent arm, but not as strong or as accurate as Nick's.

In batting practice, Dustin did okay too. He hit a few line drives. And for a right-handed hitter, he seemed to have decent power. He also hit a couple fly balls that landed right before the fence. They maybe would have been doubles in a game. But these were batting-practice pitches. The ball was coming in straight, medium speed.

In a ballgame, would Dustin be able to get around on an eighty-five-mile-an-hour fastball? Could he handle a sharp-breaking curve or a good change? Did he have a good eye for the strike zone? Was he patient enough to wait for his pitch?

Zack knew a lot of champion batting-practice hitters who couldn't keep up once the game started. He was anxious to see how Dustin did in a game situation.

Two days later Zack got his chance.

CHAPTER 7

The Roadrunners seemed to have the game in hand, leading 5–2 at home against the Kansas City Cyclones.

Zack was leaving the dugout for the on-deck circle when he heard Coach Harris tell Nick, "We're going to have Dustin hit for Kurt. Then he'll come in and catch the last two innings. We need to see how he handles himself."

Nick nodded. Zack could see Nick wasn't happy about it, but Nick was a team guy.

What the coaches said was law. And both Nick and Zack knew that's the only way a team can function.

Still, Zack wasn't happy about Coach's decision either. Five–two wasn't a safe lead against the Cyclones. In that situation, it was risky replacing Nick with a guy who hadn't even proved he could play. Zack hoped Coach Harris wasn't making a mistake.

With two outs, Zack drew a walk. Nick followed with a shot down the line in right. But the right fielder got the ball in so quickly that Wash had to hold up Zack at third. Nick eased into second.

A base hit by Dustin could stretch the lead to five runs.

"Come on, Dustin!" Zack yelled from third.

Dustin got a first pitch fastball. He came around late but made good contact, lining it foul by about twenty feet down the right-field line.

"Nice contact!" Zack shouted.

The next pitch was a sharp-breaking curve, low and away. Dustin swung and missed the ball by about two feet.

Zack moved back to third as Wash called out to Dustin, "Guard the plate now. Two strikes. Make him throw it over."

Zack doubted Wash's directions would do any good. Dustin had looked terrible swinging at that curveball. If Zack were on the mound with this pitcher's stuff, he'd throw the next pitch in the same spot. Maybe even farther outside. It would be foolish to come back with another fastball.

He just hoped Dustin could be patient. Let the curve go. Get ahead in the count. Make the pitcher have to come in with a fastball.

Zack took a big lead off third, certain it would be a curve low and outside. He just hoped the pitcher would bounce it up there. Maybe it would get past the catcher and he could plate the Roadrunners their sixth run. A three-run lead was good. Four was much better.

It was a curve. It didn't bounce.

Dustin missed it by at least a foot, and the inning was over.

Now it was up to Shotaro Mori, today's closer, to shut them down for two innings.

CHAPTER 8

After Shotaro's final warm-up pitch, Zack took Dustin's throw at second. After so many games of feeling Nick's throws slap into his mitt, it felt more like Dustin's throw was crawling into his mitt. *Not fair*, Zack thought. Maybe Nick's throws had just spoiled him. Dustin's throw really hadn't been that bad.

Zack flipped the ball to Tripp who whipped it to Nellie at third. Nellie tossed it to Shotaro.

"Be tough, Sho," Zack called out.

Nothing much happened in the eighth except for one mistake by Shotaro. The Cyclones' number-six hitter took it over the center-field fence. In their half, the Roadrunners didn't score. They still led by two going into the ninth.

Shotaro seemed rattled after a leadoff single. He kept shaking off Dustin's signs before finally walking the next batter.

Zack called time. The coaches stayed in the dugout while Zack, Nellie, Trip, and Dustin gathered around Shotaro. Gus stayed at first and chatted with the Cyclones' runner.

"Who's calling the pitches?" Zack asked.

"I am," Dustin answered.

Coach Harris and Wash were the best coaches around. They knew the game. But Zack thought they were making a mistake by not calling the pitches for Shotaro. Nick always called the pitches, but this was Dustin's first game. He didn't know the batters. He didn't know Shotaro.

"Just shake off Dustin," Zack told Shotaro, "until he gives you your pitch."

"Give me a lower target on my curve," Shotaro told Dustin. "A higher target for my fastball."

Nellie and Trip threw in their words of encouragement, and the meeting broke up.

On the second pitch, the left-handed batter hit one off the end of his bat down the left-field line. It began coming down just inches inside the line. Left fielder Darius McKay dived, appearing to be suspended in space. The ball landed in his glove just before he hit the ground. It stayed securely in his glove upon his impact with the ground. And only his world-class speed had let him make what Zack knew what was probably a game-saving catch.

The runners scampered back to second and first.

Shotaro threw three high, hard strikes past the next hitter, one called and two swinging. The Runners were one out away from a win.

Shotaro had found his rhythm. Zack knew he would use his blazing fastball to set up the next hitter. The batter swung late on the first one and fouled off the next.

Now Shotaro had him just where he wanted. Zack saw the sign for the fastball. He knew Shotaro would shake it off. He did.

Shotaro threw a sharp-breaking curve at Dustin's ankles. The batter swung and missed. Game over.

Except Dustin hadn't gotten his glove down far enough. The ball glanced off the edge of his mitt and bounded a few feet to his left. He ran over and picked it up. And the batter wasn't even half-way to first. Easy out.

But Zack couldn't believe what happened next.

Dustin threw to *third*. In spite of everybody shouting "First base!" he threw to third.

It was close, but the runner who had come from first slid in safely at third. And now the batter was safe at first, as well.

So far this season, the only thing that had kept Shotaro from being almost unhittable was his composure. He rattled easily. Nick usually knew how to calm him down.

But Nick wasn't in the game.

With runners on the corners, Shotaro still needed just one more out. But Zack could read his body language. It was saying, "I'm beat. I won't get them out."

And he didn't. Not until he'd walked the bases full, and then all three base runners scored on a base hit.

The Roadrunners went down peacefully in their half.

It was an ugly way for an eleven-game winning streak to end. And Dustin's debut had been equally ugly.

CHAPTER 9

Usually the players took their time leaving the locker room after a game. They'd joke around and talk about the game. But that wasn't the case tonight. Whatever they were thinking they kept to themselves.

Zack usually rode with Nick. Today the team's pitching ace, Carson, was also riding with them.

Carson got to the car before Zack did and promptly got into the front seat. Carson wasn't the kind of guy who was willing to take a back seat to anyone.

Nick hadn't even pulled out of the parking lot before Carson started cursing up a storm.

"What *was* that?" Carson exclaimed. "What was Coach doing? He had no business putting in the new kid when the game was on the line. Dustin cost us a game we should have won!"

"We were up three," Nick said. "We should have won anyway. It wasn't all Dustin's fault."

"Come on, man," Carson said. "If you'd been in there, we would've won. You know it."

"He's right," Zack said. "That passed ball on the strikeout. And then throwing to *third* . . ."

Nick didn't seem to have an answer for that. But Carson did. "Hasn't the guy *ever* caught a game before? Even a Little Leaguer would know enough to throw to first."

"Well, it was a shorter throw," Nick said. "He almost got him."

"But he didn't," Carson said. "I don't understand why you're defending the guy. He took over for you and cost us the game. If *you* were catching, where would have thrown the ball?"

"First base," Nick said. "You have to get the sure out."

"You know it," Carson said. "I know it. Zack back there knows it. Everybody in the freaking world knows it. Except Conover."

Nick put on his left turn signal and slowed into an intersection, waiting for the oncoming traffic to clear.

"Other than that play," Zack said, "Dustin didn't do all that bad."

Zack wasn't sure why he was defending him. Maybe he was just following Nick's lead. Or maybe it was because not long ago he had been the new guy on the Roadrunners, having to prove himself.

"You know better than that," Carson said. "What I can't figure out is why Coach brought him on board. It's pretty obvious the guy isn't travel team material."

The name Conover probably didn't mean anything to Carson. As far as Zack knew, none of the other guys knew about Pearson Hill and the Conover Stadium. They probably didn't know that Dustin's family was loaded.

But that couldn't have been the reason Dustin was a member of the Roadrunners. Coach wasn't the kind of guy who could be bought.

Was he?

. . .

Zack unlocked the apartment. His mother wouldn't be home until around midnight. She was working a late shift. Zack would probably be asleep by then. He grabbed the remote and turned on the TV. The station was already set to ESPN. He fixed himself a sandwich, poured a glass of milk, and sat down to check out the baseball scores.

They were showing the MLB web gems—the top catches of the night. Some were pretty good, slick double plays and leaping catches against the outfield fence, but none were better than the one Darius had made. His catch would have saved the game if Shotaro hadn't fallen apart. Or if Nick had still been behind the plate.

Zack's cell phone rang to the tune of his favorite Lil Wayne song. He didn't know the number that appeared on his caller ID, but he answered anyway.

"Hello."

"Hello, um, Zack? It's Dustin Conover."

Zack was surprised. Why would Dustin be calling *him*? Coach Harris made sure all the players had everybody else's cell number. If there were ever any last-minute changes in schedule, he wanted to get the word out quick.

In the locker room after the game nobody had actually gone up to Dustin and said, "You screwed up, man. Go back to where you came from and don't lose any more games for us." But on the other hand, nobody, Zack included, had said, "Shake it off. You'll do better next time."

It was almost like guys were walking over a floor covered with worms, trying to step lightly enough to keep from squishing out the worms' guts.

"Hey, Dustin," Zack said. "What's up?"

"I guess I cost us the game."

Zack was caught off guard. That's about the last thing he expected. But at least Dustin admitted it and didn't try to throw somebody else under the bus. That counted for something.

"Well, it's just too bad you didn't take the sure out at first."

"I realized that as soon as I saw the runner beat the throw to third."

"Well, next time."

"I just panicked," Dustin said.

"It was a tough spot Coach put you in, your first game and all." Zack was surprised to hear those words come out of his mouth. Their eleven-game winning streak just ended because of this guy.

Not only that, Nick was Zack's best friend on the team. And it seemed the only position Dustin played was catcher. Dustin's spot on the roster might mean less playing time for

Nick. Unless Coach decided Dustin was a liability.

"The reason I called," Dustin said, "is to see if you have any plans for tomorrow. Since we don't have a workout or a game, I hoped we could hang out."

Hang out with Dustin Conover? Why would he want to hang out with Dustin? The bigger question, though, was why would Dustin want to hang out with him? He'd only talked to the guy a few times. Sure, he'd played against him in that Pearson Hill game, but that didn't exactly make them friends or anything.

What did Dustin want from him?

CHAPTER 10

The next morning, Dustin clicked open the trunk of his car. Zack tossed his baseball equipment inside, and then he went to the front and sat in the sweetest car he'd ever been in—a silver Jaguar convertible.

"This yours?" he asked Dustin. He tried to act like he wasn't all that impressed. Like he rode in cars like this all the time.

"Yeah," Dustin said. "My dad got it for me last year when I got my driver's license. It gets me where I need to go."

"I guess it would," Zack said.

About five minutes later Dustin pulled into a Dairy Queen. "We could have lunch at my house," he said, "but I like this place. Do you mind?"

Zack didn't mind. He remembered seeing a five-dollar bill in his wallet. Enough for a hamburger at least.

"Go ahead and order first," Dustin said. When Zack ordered his hamburger, Dustin said, "That's all you're having?"

Zack shrugged.

"Get yourself some real food, man," Dustin said. "My treat."

"No," Zack said. "I've got mine." It didn't feel right, Dustin paying for his meal. He wouldn't have been able to make the same offer. Not with only five dollars.

"Look, you're my guest," Dustin said. "I invited you for lunch. So I'm paying. What kind of selfish punk would I be if I didn't?" He told Zack what he was planning to get. "I know you can eat as much as I do."

Zack hesitated for a moment and then ordered the same. It was sort of embarrassing to have Dustin pay, but it was more embarrassing to have everyone around them in line listen to this any longer.

"Thanks for the lunch," Zack said as they set their trays on a table.

"No sweat. My dad gives me an allowance." He didn't say how much. Zack didn't ask.

It turned out that Dustin lived only about four miles from Zack. Only four miles, but two planets apart. That's what it seemed to Zack anyway.

Zack had seen houses like the Conover's before. Through a car window. Or in the movies. He'd always had a hard time imagining the kind of people who lived in those houses. The small house Zack's family had lived in until his dad died would be considered the servants' quarters to people who lived in those mansions.

"You actually live here?" Zack couldn't help saying as they drove up to the house. The entire Roadrunners' team could probably live in this house and still not fill it up.

"Yeah. My dad bought it when we moved to Las Vegas. The year he enrolled me at Pearson Hill."

"You live here and go to school at Pearson Hill? That's pretty far from here."

"It's about a fifty-minute drive one way, depending on traffic. I'm used to it, though. Gives me a chance to listen to music. Now I drive myself. Up until I got my license we'd have a guy drive me there and back. I'd sit in the back-seat and do homework."

"What did the guy do who drove you?"

"What do you mean?"

"While you were in school. He didn't just sit around all day waiting, did he?"

"Oh no. He was just a driver. Dropped me off and picked me up at the end of the day."

That was crazy. Hiring your own private driver every day for years.

"This is some house," Zack said as they walked up to the front door.

"It's okay. The downstairs is the cool part."

Dustin's dad was just leaving as they walked up to the house. He looked a lot like Dustin, but with some extra weight and gray hair. He wore a suit and was rolling a black suitcase behind him. Zack couldn't recall his dad ever wearing a suit except to church.

"Hello," he said to Zack. "I'm Walter Conover, Dustin's father. I'm glad I got a chance to see you before I left."

They shook hands, and Mr. Conover turned to Dustin. "I'll be getting back from New York Friday morning. I'll be back in time to see your games this weekend. You boys have a good time, now."

He walked away. Dustin turned to go into the house. Zack walked behind him into a room unlike any he had ever seen. Each piece of furniture, each painting, each little sculpture must have cost more than all the furnishings and objects in all the houses Zack had ever lived in put together.

"I'm surprised your dad has enough money left over to give you an allowance," Zack said.

"Yeah, he's CEO of NZRCORP. That's why he's going to New York. Another meeting. Counting stocks and options, he makes more than fourteen mil a year. That's why he has to go to New York a lot. And that's why he can afford to give me an allowance."

The strange thing was, Zack was positive Dustin wasn't bragging. He was just stating a fact. The way somebody might say, "They're paying me seven dollars an hour working as a cashier."

Fourteen million.

Zack had to wonder once again what he was doing there.

And that was before he saw the downstairs.

CHAPTER 11

"You've really got to see his house," Zack told Nick as they drove to practice the next morning.

"Nice?" Nick said.

"Look," Zack said. "I love your house. You live in one of the nicest houses I've ever been in. But Dustin's house. It's something else, man."

He tried to describe the Conovers' house and landscape and view. But he knew he couldn't possibly do it justice.

He did a little better describing the swimming pool. Because although he didn't know exactly what an Olympic-size swimming pool looked like, he knew that the Conovers' pool could probably give one a good run for its money.

He did best with the downstairs. The game room, exercise center, entertainment center, and library. Maybe it wasn't as large as a football field, but it sure felt that way.

"He has a batting cage with a pitching machine at one end of it. I mean, it's a first-class pitching machine. In his *basement*, man! You can adjust speeds. Make it throw curves at any speed."

"Does he use it?" Nick asked.

Zack knew what Nick meant by that. Dustin sure hadn't looked comfortable swinging at curveballs for the Runners.

"That's the thing. When I had it set for curveballs, no matter what speed, he hit them good. If he knew it was going to be a curve, that is. But when he didn't know what pitch was coming, he was lost. It's almost like he's afraid of the ball. His mind is already telling his body to back away."

"Oh yeah?

"Yeah, and he told me he needed me to help him."

"You?"

"I know. Why me? I'm one of the worst hitters on the Roadrunners."

"Oh, I wouldn't say that," Nick said.

"Really?"

Nick laughed. "Okay. Maybe I would."

"Thanks," Zack muttered.

"So what did he mean, he wants your help?"

Zack shrugged. "I told him his dad should hire a professional batting coach to work with him. Lots of guys on our team have done that. He said he's had a couple. They helped. Right now he's between coaches. Whatever that means. He said he still has trouble with the curve."

"No kidding."

"I mean, it's crazy. It's the first time I talked to the guy for more than a couple minutes at a time. He has me go to his house and asks me to be his hitting instructor. Go figure."

Nick shook his head. "It sounds crazy, all right."

"He said to me, 'You know the game. And I trust you.' What's that supposed to mean, anyway?"

Nick grinned. "I guess it means he trusts you to turn against your buddy Nick and help him take away my starting job."

"Like that'll ever happen."

Nick shrugged.

CHAPTER 12

The Roadrunners hosted the Seattle Thunder in a doubleheader that afternoon. The Runners seemed stronger at almost every position. But the beauty of baseball is that whichever team plays better on a given day usually wins.

The Roadrunners played better in game one. They scored seven runs in the first three innings against Greg Marin, a right-hander who was supposed to be the Thunder's ace.

They then tacked on four more runs off of two Thunder relievers in an 11–2 win.

Coach Harris apparently felt this would be another good chance to give Dustin some game experience, so he started him behind the plate in game two. Not everybody was happy about it, especially Carson, the game-two pitcher.

Between games, Trip came over to Zack. "Did you hear about where the money for the trip to New York came from?"

"I heard," Zack said, "that most of it probably came from Carson's dad." By now everyone sort of assumed that Carson's dad had been the one to foot the bill. Even Carson himself had hinted to it. Zack wouldn't have been surprised. Carson's family had a lot of money and didn't mind showing it.

But Trip shook his head. "That's what Carson would want everybody to believe. But it's not true. It came from Mr. Conover."

"You're kidding . . ."

"Not at all." Trip lowered his voice. "The story that's going around is that Conover has his own plane big enough to fly our whole team to New York. And he's going to pay for our hotel and food."

"What's Carson say about that?"

"I think Carson's ticked off. He's used to being the one with the most money, but I think Dustin has him beat now."

Zack shrugged. He'd never really thought too much about who on the team had money and who didn't. Trip had a wealthy family too. His dad was a pretty famous singer.

"I hope Carson keeps his head in the game," Zack said finally. "He doesn't much like Dustin anyway. And with Dustin catching him . . ."

"Man, it could be a disaster," Trip said.

"Coach must know what he's doing."

"Let's hope so," Trip said.

. . .

Carson got the first two outs easily on a strikeout and a pop fly to short right field. Then the trouble started.

He got a quick strike on the third batter. His second pitch was a high fastball. The ball glanced off the top of Dustin's mitt and clanked against Dustin's mask so hard that it knocked him backward.

While Coach and Wash rushed from the dugout to check on Dustin, Zack looked at Carson. A slight smile peeked out from under Carson's cap as he studied the ground. Before Zack had time to think, he found himself running out to the pitcher's mound.

"What's with that?" Zack asked when he approached Carson. He was trying to stay clam. This wasn't really his battle. "Dustin called for a curve."

"He signaled fastball," Carson said.

"Man, I saw the signal as clearly as you did."

"He put down two fingers."

"I saw what I saw. And you saw it too. You deliberately crossed him up."

"Just go back and do your job," Carson said. "Let me do mine."

"Just don't cross him up again."

"Go worry about playing second base. I'll pitch the ball," Carson repeated.

Zack glared at Carson. "Don't lose the ballgame for us just because you're jealous of Dustin."

Dustin was walking toward the mound. Coach Harris and Wash were headed for the dugout. Zack wondered if they knew Dustin had been crossed up. Zack started backing toward his position. He didn't want Dustin to know he'd been defending him.

"I called for a curve," Zack heard Dustin say in a matter-of-fact tone as Zack headed back.

"Sorry," Carson said. "I thought I saw two fingers."

"No. I just put down one."

"Make sure it's clear next time. I thought it was two."

Zack didn't hear anymore. But a few seconds later Dustin went back to the plate. The batter went out on the next pitch, a curve on the outside corner at the knees. Dustin handled it cleanly.

On the other side of the ball, Dustin struggled with his hitting. In the second inning with two outs, Zack worked the Thunder's pitcher for a walk. Then Dustin was up. On the second pitch, Zack stole second base. Leading off from second, he had a good look at the next pitches. The Thunder's pitcher wasn't throwing hard, but with two strikes he curved Dustin inside. He almost fell away from the plate. The ball came back and caught the inside corner. Zack didn't think it was an especially good curve. It was the kind of pitch good hitters hammer hard every time. But Dustin couldn't even swing because he already had his butt out of the batter's box.

It really looked like he was afraid of the ball.

On the field, the game turned even worse for Dustin. In the third inning, Carson threw twenty-three pitches. After the inning ended, Zack sat in the dugout going back over the pitches. He remembered each one. Carson must have shaken off Dustin on at least half of them. And a walk and two base hits had given the Thunder the first run of the game.

This wasn't a pitcher and catcher working together. It was a one-sided war, with a pitcher trying to take down his catcher. The catcher was just trying to survive.

CHAPTER 13

The Roadrunners exploded on offense for four runs in the fourth to give Carson a cushion. He needed it.

On defense in the fifth, two sharp-breaking curveballs in the dirt got past Dustin on consecutive pitches, moving a runner from first to third. Both pitches were scored as passed balls, though Zack felt they could easily have been scored as wild pitches.

Still, he had to admit: Nick probably would

have blocked them.

After that inning, when neither Coach Harris nor Wash was within hearing range, Carson muttered in the dugout to Dustin, "Have to stick with fastballs. Don't dare throw my curve." Dustin didn't respond. He just turned away.

Zack was sitting next to Nick. "Those were tough pitches to handle," he said. Nick just shrugged and kept quiet.

The Roadrunners added four more runs. Coach Harris took out Carson after seven innings. He'd only given up three runs, but it looked as if he was on the verge of giving up more.

The Thunder had stolen two bases. Zack thought they were really stolen on Carson. He had let the runners get big leads off the bag, and he hadn't made any effort to hold them close. It was almost as if he had wanted them to steal. The catcher usually takes the blame when a runner steals against him. Dustin was the scapegoat. It was pretty clear by now that Carson was sabotaging Dustin.

The Thunder added two more runs off Jose Diaz in the final two innings. The Roadrunners won 8–5, but they played with no enthusiasm. It was almost as if they were just going through the motions, watching the game as if it were some kind of soap opera. They seemed to be more interested in what would happen with Dustin than they were with the game itself.

Going 0 for 4, Dustin hadn't performed any better at the plate than he had behind it. Meanwhile, Nick got in the game only as a pinch hitter, lacing a single to left before watching the rest of the game on the bench.

Zack wondered how long it would be before Coach Harris would admit that Dustin's presence on the team was already creating some problems. And for the second time Zack had to consider: was Coach playing Dustin only because of Mr. Conover's money?

On the ride home with Nick, Zack gave Nick a good opportunity to badmouth Dustin. He thought he might need to get it off his chest. After all, Nick had spent most of the game on the bench because of Dustin.

"Dustin didn't look real good out there," Zack started.

"Well, we won," Nick said. "That's the important thing."

"Yeah," Zack said. "But still, we barely beat a team that isn't very good. What will happen when we come up against a top team?"

Nick had the right to be mad, but all he said was, "It's a long season. Coach and Wash are good coaches. They'll get it figured out."

Sure they will, Zack thought. *But when?*

...

That night, Trip invited a bunch of the guys over to play poker at his house and to swim in his pool. Zack wasn't surprised to see almost the entire team there—except Dustin.

Trip had a really nice, big house, but it looked like a shack compared to Dustin's mansion. Still, the guys had a good time playing poker over there. They never bet any money. It was just for fun.

As the night grew later, only Nellie, Zack, and Nick remained. They floated in the pool, sipping lemonade. Zack was finally relaxed, staring up at the night sky.

"We've got to talk to Coach," Nellie finally said.

"What?" Zack said.

"Look, I don't want to be a jerk, but Dustin playing and Nick sitting? You know that's not right. "

Zack glanced at Nick. He was sipping his lemonade but looking away.

"Well, yeah," Zack said. "Of course Nick should be out there. But it's only been one game."

"Two games," Nellie said. "He cost us one."

"But Harris is the coach," Zack said. "That's like mutiny, trying to tell a coach who should play and who shouldn't."

"It's not just that. You've heard the rumor. That Dustin's dad *bought* his way on the team.

The only reason he's here is because his dad's paying for our New York trip."

"Yeah, I've heard that," Zack admitted.

"I was talking to some of the guys tonight. Since I'm team captain they asked me to talk to Coach. But I think he'll be more likely to listen if a couple of us go in. Like maybe . . . the three of us."

Nick finally spoke, "Not me. No way I'm gonna tell Coach what to do on this."

"We have to think of what is best for the team here," Nellie said.

"Sorry," Nick said. "You're on your own."

"How about it, Zack? Tomorrow morning before practice? You understand the game better than just about anybody. He'll listen to you."

"Hey, I'm new on this team. You think I want to get Coach mad? No way."

"We need to find out exactly why Dustin is playing. Or our whole season might be in jeopardy."

"I don't know, man." Of course, Nellie had a point. But Zack was sure Coach had his reasons for playing Dustin. He just hoped it wasn't all about the money.

"I'm just thinking of the good of the team," Nellie insisted. "Do you wait until a house burns down before you call the fire department, or do you call at the first sign of flames?"

"It's not the same thing," Zack said. Nellie wasn't usually so dramatic. He must have been really worried about this.

"Look." Nellie set his empty lemonade glass by the edge of the pool. "More than anything I just want to know if the rumor is true."

"Yeah, me too," Nick piped up again. "But I'm *not* talking to Coach."

"Okay," Zack finally said. "I don't like it, but I'll go with you, Nellie."

CHAPTER 14

The next morning, while most of the guys were getting ready for practice, Nellie and Zack went to talk to Coach Harris. Zack's stomach was flip-flopping uncomfortably. He usually made it a rule not question the Coach's calls, but this seemed important. He hoped it was the right decision.

Nellie knocked on the door to the coaches' office. Both Coach and Wash were still there.

"Have you got a minute?" Nellie asked.

"Let me guess," Coach Harris said. "It's about Dustin."

Nellie nodded. Zack wasn't at all surprised that Coach already knew why they were there. He was a smart guy.

Coach Harris motioned for them to take a chair. "You've heard the rumor."

Zack said, "We heard that Mr. Conover is paying for our New York trip . . . So, um, I guess we are wondering . . . is that why Dustin is on the team?"

The two coaches exchanged looks. Wash said, "That's partly it. But it's not as simple as that. You fellas know Coach Harris and I always do what's best for the team and you boys."

Nellie said, "Dustin has already cost us one game and almost another one. We think Nick should be playing."

Coach Harris took off his cap and ran a hand through his silver hair. "Our sponsors did everything they could, but there still wasn't enough money for the New York trip. That was when Walter Conover said if we could find room on our roster for Dustin, he'd provide the funds we needed. But understand this: we didn't make any concessions that would weaken our team. I only assured him we'd try to get Dustin some playing time. We wouldn't have taken him, New York trip or not, if we felt it would hurt the team."

"Maybe," Nellie said, "but he's not Nick."

"I'm not disagreeing," Coach Harris said. "I shouldn't have put Dustin in before he was ready. It wasn't fair to him or to the team. I'm going to be more careful in how I use him moving forward. We can make Dustin a better player, and he and his family can help us. His being here is helping you already by making it possible to play in the New York tournament. In fact, it would be great if you guys could do some work with Dustin rather than coming in here to complain about him."

"What about Nick?" Zack spat out before he lost his nerve completely.

"Don't worry about that," Coach Harris said. "If Nick is concerned, you tell him to talk to me."

When they left the office, Zack felt a little better. Coach Harris wasn't really selling out. If Dustin was used in ways that would help Dustin develop as a player, not cost the team any more games, and allow the team to get to New York—that couldn't be anything but good.

Could it?

. . .

In the next four games, Dustin was used as a pinch hitter twice and was behind the plate for only four innings at the end of two one-sided games. And Zack had decided to help Dustin like Coach had suggested. They worked out together during week.

One Thursday evening, Zack and Dustin were at Dustin's working out in his downstairs batting cage. Zack kept giving Dustin all the advice he knew.

"Don't back out."

"When it starts to break, slap it to right."

"Don't try to pull everything."

"Step up in the box against a curveball pitcher. Get the pitch before it breaks."

"Study the pitcher's pattern. Sometimes you can predict when he's most likely to curve you."

He knew he wasn't telling Dustin anything he probably hadn't already heard from other coaches. But he hoped all this practice would have some effect on Dustin's performance.

While they were done, Dustin opened the door of the small refrigerator where he kept sodas and Gatorade.

"All out of cold Gatorade. You mind running upstairs and seeing if there's any in the fridge?"

"Sure, man."

Zack ran up the stairs two at a time. He had to pass Mr. Conover's study on the way to the kitchen. Zack stopped short when he heard Mr. Conover's angry voice through the open study door.

"Harris, listen to me."

Zack didn't want to eavesdrop, but he

didn't dare move for fear Mr. Conover might hear him and think he was listening.

He couldn't help but overhear what Mr. Conover was saying.

CHAPTER 15

"I know what I promised," Mr. Conover said. "But you knew the deal from the beginning. You were going to help Dustin develop into major-league material. He can't do that sitting on the bench. He has to start."

After a brief pause, Mr. Conover said, "I'm sorry if you misunderstood. But if Dustin is not your full-time starting catcher within the next week, you'll have to find a different way to fund your New York trip."

More afraid now that Mr. Conover might step out of his study and see him, Zack turned and walked quietly back down the stairs. Once at the bottom he called out, for Mr. Conover's benefit, not Dustin's, "I'm going up for the Gatorade!"

He ran noisily up the stairs, and then he walked to the kitchen. Mr. Conover was shuffling through some papers on his desk with his back to the door when Zack walked past his study.

What to do now? This was the big problem.

Zack had been at Dustin's house almost every day they didn't have a team workout or game. Zack actually really liked Dustin. He was a cool guy, and he was willing to work hard to be on the team. Zack respected that. Yet Zack still considered Nick to be his best friend of anyone on the team. Now, Nick's position as starting catcher was on the line.

Zack felt caught in the middle. By working with Dustin, was he undermining Nick? If Zack helped Dustin get good enough, maybe

Coach Harris would feel the team wouldn't be hurt that much by having Dustin behind the plate full-time. And what about the team? Right now, Nick was still more valuable to the team than Dustin.

Yet that New York tournament was also important. It would give all of them a chance to be seen by dozens of pro scouts and representatives from colleges. Their futures in baseball might be directly affected by playing in that tournament.

Zack grabbed two Gatorades from the fridge and walked back down to the basement.

"What's up?" Dustin said. "You look bummed out about something. I thought we both hit the ball good today."

Zack forced a smile. "We did, for sure. I'm just worn out."

"How about a swim?" Dustin said.

"You got it."

Then suddenly a new thought entered Zack's mind—did Dustin *know* about his dad's arrangement with Coach Harris? Dustin had to notice that he didn't play as well as the other Runners. But Zack didn't think Dustin would put himself before the team.

On the other hand, though, Dustin knew that Nick was Zack's friend. Is that why he picked Zack out of all of the other better hitters on the Roadrunners to work with him?

CHAPTER 16

The way Zack looked at it, every game was a big one. But everybody else was talking about the upcoming four-team invitational tournament in Phoenix, Arizona, as being one of the biggest of the season so far. The Roadrunners would be up against three other top travel teams in the Southeast: the Phoenix Lions, the Albuquerque Terriers, and the Salt Lake City Bobcats.

If they could win this tournament, the

Roadrunners would show the nation that they were truly one of the country's elite teams. It would certainly improve their chances of getting a high seed at New York.

Phoenix was an almost six-hour drive from Las Vegas. The team would be staying two nights in a hotel. On Friday evening, the Roadrunners would play the Bobcats. The Terriers would take on the Lions. On Saturday afternoon, the game one winners would play each other, and the game one losers would play each other. The two teams with one loss would then play each other on Sunday. And the winner of that game would play for the championship against the team that had won both of its games.

The team that won its first two games would have a big edge. It would have to play only one game on Sunday to win the championship, not two. Having to play four games in three days would stretch a pitching staff pretty thin.

Zack was catching a ride home from practice the day before the tournament when Nick gave him the news.

"Coach called Dustin and me into his office after practice."

"Yeah, I saw," Zack said. "What was that about?"

"Coach expects Mattullo to start for the Bobcats. If he does, Dustin will be starting catcher. Kurt will throw for us."

"What? The biggest game of the year so far and he's not putting you behind the plate?"

"He said Mattullo throws ninety percent fastballs. So this will be a good match-up for Dustin, not having to worry about the curve."

"That doesn't make any sense. You murder fastballs." Zack thought about the conversation between Mr. Conover and Coach Harris. He felt sick. Zack had told Nick about his and Nellie's talk with Coach about Dustin, but so far he'd kept quiet about what he'd overheard at Dustin's house.

"You know me. I'm a team guy," Nick said. "I do what Coach says unless there's a really good reason not to. But I want to win. We've got a better chance to win with me in there. Not bragging. Just stating a fact."

"This isn't right," Zack said. "We have to beat the Bobcats."

"We can still win the tourney, even if we lose the first one. We can win our next three."

"If you're in the lineup for the next three we can," Zack said. "Maybe Coach thinks going to New York is more important than winning this tourney, though. What if he decides to go with Dustin all the way?"

Nick didn't answer. Zack could only guess at what he might have been thinking.

Zack understood that Coach Harris was in a tight spot. But was the New York tournament really worth benching one of your best players, a guy who might just be one of the best seventeen-year-old catchers in the country? The odds of losing jumped up considerably with an unproven catcher with less than half of Nick's experience starting in. Living in Las Vegas, Zack and all the Runners knew something about odds.

Zack couldn't take it any longer. He had to tell Nick what he knew.

"Look, I think I know what's going on,"

Zack said. "Mr. Conover told Coach he wouldn't pay for the New York trip unless Dustin was the Roadrunners' *starting* catcher."

Nick's eyes widened. "You know this how?"

"I heard Mr. Conover on the phone with Coach when I was at Dustin's house. I don't think Dustin knows."

"How could he not know?"

Zack shook his head. "He's a good guy. He works hard. I think he cares about the team. I really don't think he'd want to buy his way to a starting spot."

"This is bad. Zack, I really need my spot on the team . . ." For the first time since Dustin joined the team, Zack saw real concern in his friend's eyes.

"I'm thinking I should let Nellie know," Zack said. "We can't keep something like this from our captain. You know, except for Mr. Conover, we all want the same things."

"Which are?"

"Everybody wants to win. Everybody wants *you* in the lineup. Everybody wants to go to New York."

Nick said, "Well it looks like everybody isn't going to get everything they want. New York's coming up soon. Coach isn't likely to pull the plug on it now."

"If we fall behind early or if Dustin is killing us behind the plate, Coach won't wait long."

"Let's hope it doesn't come to that."

• • •

There were a lot of surprised looks when Coach Harris named Dustin as starting catcher for the Bobcats game before the team left Las Vegas that morning.

Zack was planning to sit by Nick on the bus, but Nick was instead hanging out in Shotaro's family's RV. Usually, parents and other family members caravanned with the team's bus. A lot of the players' families had RVs that were even nicer than the team's deluxe coach bus.

With Nick absent from the seats next to Zack, Dustin took a seat nearby.

Zack was trying to kick back and listen to his iPod when he felt someone poke him in the ribs. It was Dustin. Zack pulled out his earbuds.

"What's up, man?"

"Is Nick hurt?" Dustin said in a low voice.

"Uh, no, there's nothing wrong with him. He's in Sho's RV."

"Okay . . ." Dustin settled back in his seat as if that was all he had to say, but suddenly he again leaned toward Zack. "So why isn't Nick starting in the Bobcats game?"

Zack finally had his answer. Dustin *didn't* know about his father's arrangement with Coach. This was Zack's chance to tell Dustin the truth, but he hesitated. It wasn't really his battle to fight. It was between Dustin and his dad. And Dustin would find out eventually.

"Well, uh, Coach is probably just going to save Nick for the right moment." Zack finally said.

Dustin smiled and gave Zack a fist-bump. "Alright, cool, man."

Zack frowned as his new friend smiled while gazing out the bus window. He almost wished there was no such thing as the big New York tournament. As much as he liked Dustin, Zack wished he'd never heard of Walter Conover and his private plane.

CHAPTER 17

When they got to the hotel, there was little time to explore the hotel's amenities: the indoor swimming pool, the exercise room, the game room with its video games and pool tables, and the spa, before the team dinner at 6:00. The Roadrunners would be playing the Bobcats at 10:00 in the morning, and Coach had set an 11:00 P.M. lights-out. But Zack hoped he'd at least have time to take advantage of his room's free Wii.

And maybe he'd even be able to sneak in a soak in the huge whirlpool bathtub before lights-out.

Zack was rooming with Dustin. When Zack had expressed amazement at the hotel and at their room, Dustin hadn't. Zack realized that Dustin had probably stayed in hotels like this many times before. On the few occasions when Zack had traveled with his parents, they had always stayed at the cheapest motel they could find—the kind where his mother had to inspect the room to make sure no bugs were crawling around.

The team had reserved a room in the hotel restaurant for the team dinner. Most of the players seemed in high spirits, even after the long day of travel. *And what is not to enjoy?* Zack thought. If he had ever eaten at a restaurant so—what was the word, elegant?—he couldn't remember when.

Throughout the meal, while he was enjoying the thickest, most tender steak he'd ever eaten, Zack kept catching Nellie's eyes boring into him. He shot him a look like,

"What?" but Nellie looked away.

Dustin was quiet. He seemed distracted, as if his mind was far from food and conversation. Zack hadn't yet had a chance to talk to him about the arrangement his father had made with Coach Harris.

Before they left the restaurant, Nellie whispered to Zack, "Come to our room at eight o'clock. We need to talk." Nellie was sharing a room with Nick.

• • •

When Zack and Dustin got back to their room after dinner, Zack had to rush over to meet Nellie. He was sure Nellie wanted to talk about Dustin again.

But he couldn't make it out the door before Dustin said, "It's not right."

"What's not right?" Zack said.

Dustin clicked the remote and the TV came on. Dustin found ESPN, but he kept the volume on mute. "I've been thinking. I know the guys don't like that I'm catching instead of

Nick. And I don't blame them. I'm not as good as Nick. Not yet, anyway."

"Then why do you think Coach has you back there instead of Nick?"

"Probably for the experience. But in a tournament like this we need our best guy. That's Nick. Don't get me wrong. I'd love to be the starting catcher, if I was the best one the team had. But I'm not. My dad keeps telling me I'm better than Nick, but I know I'm not."

"You're a good catcher," Zack said. "You've got a good arm. You can drive the fastball."

Dustin smiled. "Yeah. But I can hear a 'but' coming."

Zack grinned back. "*But* Nick has a great arm. He can hit everything. And he's had more experience handling pitchers. As hard as you're working, though, you might be as good as Nick someday."

"But not today," Dustin said. "We agree on that. So tomorrow Nick needs to catch." Suddenly, Dustin looked sort of angry.

"I don't get this Harris guy," Dustin grumbled. "If I were him, I wouldn't be using my sloppy, second-string catcher for a tournament like this"

"Man, you're not sloppy. You're working on it." Zack insisted.

But Dustin just shrugged. After a minute he said, "Gonna play the Wii. Want to?"

"Sure. But I've gotta go check on something with Nick first. I'll be back in a bit."

"Sure, man."

. . .

When Zack got to Nick and Nellie's room, Carson was there too.

The first thing Nellie said when he opened the door for Zack was, "This has gone far enough. We need Nick behind the plate. This is a serious tournament. We need to win."

"I know," Zack said. "So what next?"

"We told Carson why Dustin is catching," Nick said.

"Look," Carson said. "I want to go to New York as much as anybody. I want the scouts to see my stuff. But I want to win my game tomorrow. I can't do it if I have to pitch to Dustin."

"I want to win too," Zack snapped. "We all do. But we can't win if you're on the mound crying because you don't have the catcher you want."

"Listen here, Waddell," Carson said, taking a step toward him.

"No. You listen," Zack said. "Obviously, Nick is the better catcher. But if Coach wants to have Dustin back there a little longer so we can go to New York, we just have to make sure we win with Dustin."

Nick said, "Zack's right. Once we get to New York, things will get back to normal."

"Easy for you to say," Carson said. "You don't have to try pitching to a guy who doesn't even know how to call a game or catch a curveball in the dirt."

"He's getting better," Zack said.

Carson snorted. "Not good enough."

"Look." Nellie got between Zack and Carson. "Zack, maybe you can talk to Dustin tonight. Just let him know the team doesn't like this whole blackmail thing he and his dad are pulling."

"Blackmail?" Zack said.

"Well . . . what else would you call it?" Nellie said. "I mean his dad is using *money* to get Coach to start him. That's just wrong."

"Okay, maybe it is," Zack said. "But Dustin doesn't know anything about it."

"Wow, are you sure?" Nick said.

"I'm sure."

"Well," Nellie said, "it's time *somebody* told him."

"Look, man," Zack said. "No way. I'm not doing it." Zack marched to the door. This was ridiculous. He wasn't going to be the one to crush Dustin completely. It wasn't his battle to fight.

"Come on, man," Nellie called after Zack as he entered the hallway. Zack just ignored him, but as he turned to start down the hall he saw a slumping figure walking away from him, just ten feet ahead. It was Dustin.

Had he heard? Zack wondered.

"Hey, man!" Zack called after him. But Dustin didn't even turn around. He just waved his hand out at his side in a dismissive greeting.

Then Zack knew—Dustin had heard every word.

CHAPTER 18

Since Dustin didn't seem like he wanted to be followed, Zack hung out in the hotel game room until it was almost time for lights-out. When Zack got back to the room, Dustin was already asleep. And in the morning, he didn't say a word to Zack. Zack wasn't sure who Dustin was really mad at—his dad for blackmailing the team or Zack for keeping quiet about the whole thing.

• • •

The game against the Bobcats was still scoreless in the second inning when Dustin came up to bat with two outs. Danny was on second, and Zack was on first.

"Come on, Dustin!" Zack called out. "Look for your pitch!" He took a good lead at first. With a runner on second, the first baseman wasn't holding him on.

Zack knew if Dustin played a good game it would make it easier for Coach Harris to justify keeping Dustin as starting catcher and keeping Nick on the bench. But Zack couldn't worry about that now. All he needed to worry about was the Roadrunners getting some runs.

Dustin took a high fastball for ball one. The second pitch was another fastball on the outside part of the plate. Dustin swung late and popped up a foul out of play. Coach Harris had been right. Mattullo was throwing mostly fastballs. But they were in the high 80s, maybe even in the 90s. Not easy to hit, even if you knew one was coming.

The third pitch was another fastball, this one at the knees. Dustin hit it square and golfed it into right center, splitting the two outfielders. Zack was off with contact. He scored easily, but as he jogged to the dugout, smiling, he realized something was happening on the field.

Looking back onto the field, Zack saw Dustin. He was in between first and second, wincing, with his left leg lifted off the ground. Zack had seen it enough times in baseball to guess what was going on—a pulled hamstring. Wash helped Dustin off the field while a few people in the stands and everyone in the Runners' dugout cheered for the rookie player.

In the dugout, Coach and the trainer examined Dustin's injury.

"Can you straighten your leg?" the trainer asked.

Dustin tried, but winced.

The trainer frowned, "Hamstring. I'm sure of it."

"Nick, you're in," Coach said.

Nick leapt up from the bench like a

firefighter at the sound of an alarm. He rushed to warm up.

With Nick back in the game, the entire team seemed reenergized. And Nick stayed true to the team's expectations. In the seventh inning, Nick drove in a perfect run with a single.

For the first time in a while, Nick had stayed in for almost a complete game. The Roadrunners won 5–2, with Nick driving in three of the five runs. He'd done a spectacular job behind the plate too.

As the Runners celebrated their win in the dugout, Zack noticed that Dustin was smiling as big as anyone, even though he didn't get to play most of the game. It was then that Zack knew—there was *nothing* wrong with Dustin's hamstring.

• • •

"You're a team man," Zack told Dustin that night back at the hotel. "I knew it." They were playing Wii in their hotel room, and Dustin had explained his plan to fake an injury. If he couldn't play, Coach could use Nick without Dustin's father pulling the funding for the New York trip.

"I understand why you didn't tell me about my dad," Dustin said. "But I wasn't going to let the team lose a big game like this because of me."

"Yeah," Zack agreed. "But there's still a problem."

"What?"

"If you don't see any game time, you'll never get any better."

"I know."

"So . . ."

"So, yeah, I've gotta talk to my dad. I know." Dustin frowned.

"And come clean with Coach. What if we need you to hit or something?"

"Yeah, right."

CHAPTER 19

The Terriers beat the Lions in their Friday game. Then, because they'd both lost their Friday games, the Bobcats played the Lions on Saturday. While waiting for their own Saturday game to get underway, the Roadrunners saw most of the Bobcats–Lions game. The Bobcats won easily, 14–3. In the process, they were able to save two good starting pitchers for the following day's games, knowing they'd have to win two, no matter which teams they played.

If the Roadrunners beat the Terriers today, they'd have to win only one game on Sunday. If they lost to the Terriers, they'd have to beat both the Bobcats and the Terriers on Sunday.

With Nick back in as catcher and Carson on the mound, the Roadrunners' battle against the Terriers started out in their favor. However, the Terriers had serious power hitters, and before long they pulled ahead of the Runners. In the dugout, Dustin iced his hamstring. And eventually, the Terriers beat the Runners by two. Now they would have to beat both the Bobcats and the Terriers to win the tournament.

• • •

On Sunday, while they got ready for the Bobcats game in the locker room, Dustin whispered to Nick, "Talked to my dad."

"Good. What happened?"

"He's mad. Thinks I'm making a big mistake. He said the point of having so much money is that it gives you certain advantages." Dustin shrugged.

"You believe that?" Zack was a little afraid to hear the answer.

"Seems like a crappy way to make friends," Dustin said. "I told him I wasn't going to start again until Coach asks me to. In the end, he promised to stay out of it."

"And New York?"

"We're going, no matter who's starting."

Zack smiled. "Did you tell Coach yet?"

Dustin headed for the door, giving his best fake limp. "I will."

. . .

Nick broke the Bobcats' spirit early with a three-run homer in the second inning. That's all Carson needed. He no-hit the Bobcats until the fifth, and even then they didn't score. The Roadrunners added a fourth run in the sixth inning. And Carson went the distance, scattering three more hits but no runs in a 4–0 win, sending them to the championship game against the Terriers.

Dustin hadn't seen any action in the game.

Zack kept waiting, hoping to see him talk with Coach, but he just sat there.

Zack couldn't help but notice Mr. Conover's solemn expression from his spot behind the screen in back of home plate. To say he didn't look happy would be an understatement. But at least, as far as Zack could tell, he didn't make any effort to try to make Coach Harris put Dustin in the game. Of course, Dustin had the "injury" to consider.

But Zack wasn't going to worry about that now. He and the rest of the team didn't even have time to bask in the elation of their 4–0 win. They had only another half an hour before their championship game against the Terriers.

The Terriers would be well rested. The Roadrunners would not.

Kurt Kinnard would be on the mound for the Roadrunners. The Terriers would be going with their ace, Sky Dennison. Even with Nick behind the plate for another nine innings, the Roadrunners had a hard road ahead of them.

CHAPTER 20

Things looked bad for the Roadrunners at the start of the final game of the tournament. Sky Dennison put down Darius, Gus, and Nellie in order in the top of the first. In the bottom half, Kurt seemed to be pressing. Zack figured it was because he knew Sky wasn't going to give up many runs, so he couldn't afford to either. Zack knew that wasn't a good way for a pitcher to think.

Kurt was aiming his pitches. And before Nick could get him settled down, he'd walked two batters and thrown a pitch so wild even Nick couldn't stop it. That advanced both runners.

With runners on second and third, Kurt got the number-three hitter to pop out to Gus. But his first pitch to their cleanup hitter got too much of the plate. Two runs scored on the line single to left.

Kurt settled down, but the damage had been done.

All of the Roadrunners went down meekly at their first at bats. Dennison's blazing fastball, sharp-breaking curve, and deceptive change seemed to have them overmatched, which was something that almost never happened with the Roadrunners.

In the fourth inning, though, the Roadrunners fought back. Even though the third baseman was looking bunt, Darius laid down a perfect one and beat a good throw to first by a step. Every run was important, so Zack wasn't surprised when Wash again gave

Gus the bunt sign. The strategy worked. It moved Darius to second, where he'd be able to score on a single.

Next up, Nellie did better than that. He took advantage of a rare Dennison mistake—a fastball out over the plate. Nellie drove it over the left center-field fence to tie the game.

Dustin was leading the cheers from the bench.

It was still 2–2 in the ninth when Dennison suddenly had trouble finding the plate. With one out he walked Danny, but then struck out Zack. Then walked Nick on four straight balls. While the Terrier coach went to the mound to settle down Sky, Coach Harris looked for a pinch hitter. He called on Kurt. Kurt wasn't a solid hitter, but he was the best option they had.

"Okay, Kurt," Coach Harris said. "Nice and easy now. We need a good hit to get these guy off our backs."

Kurt looked nervous. While he was steady at the mound, at the plate his nerves could cause him to fall apart.

Then Zack remembered all the work he'd been doing with Dustin in the batting cage. Dustin was a more solid choice than Kurt.

Zack leaned down to Dustin, who was still keeping up the act, icing his hamstring.

"Man, you've gotta speak up," Zack whispered. "You can hit off this guy. I know you can. You've been studying this pitcher all game."

"No way," Dustin said. "You know the team is sick of my mistakes. They are all *happy* I'm not playing."

"Yeah, but they shouldn't be," Zack said. "Give them a reason to be bummed you're *not* playing. Come on."

Meanwhile, Dennison got Trip to pop out. Whoever batted next could be the Runners' last shot.

Suddenly, Dustin jumped up. "Coach! I've got to talk to you."

. . .

From the dugout, Zack watched Dustin at the plate. Coach had not been at all pleased with Dustin's fake injury, but he too knew the team's chances were better with Dustin than with Kurt.

Dustin looked more confident than ever. Most of the team had heard his confession in the dugout, and most knew what he'd sacrificed for them.

Zack knew that Dustin's job was to take a pitch in that situation. Sky had walked two batters, so Dustin had to try to draw a walk as well. Dustin did take the first pitch—a strike. Zack panicked. It seemed like Dennison had found his location again.

But on the next pitch, Dustin took an amazing swing at the first pitch and drove it into the gap in left-center. Nick and Danny scored. The Roadrunners were tournament champions.

Dustin raced back to the dugout as the ballpark exploded with cheers. The Roadrunners patted Dustin on the back while Zack reached out and shook his hand.

"Welcome to the Runners, man."

ABOUT THE AUTHOR

Gene Fehler's ten published books include two novels: *Beanball* (Clarion Books, 2008) and *Never Blame the Umpire* (Zonderkidz, 2010). Society of School Librarians International named *Beanball* the 2008 Best Book, Grades 7–12 Novels. His *Change-Up: Baseball Poems* (Clarion Books, 2009) won the 2010 Paterson Prize for Best Book for Young People, Grades 4–6.

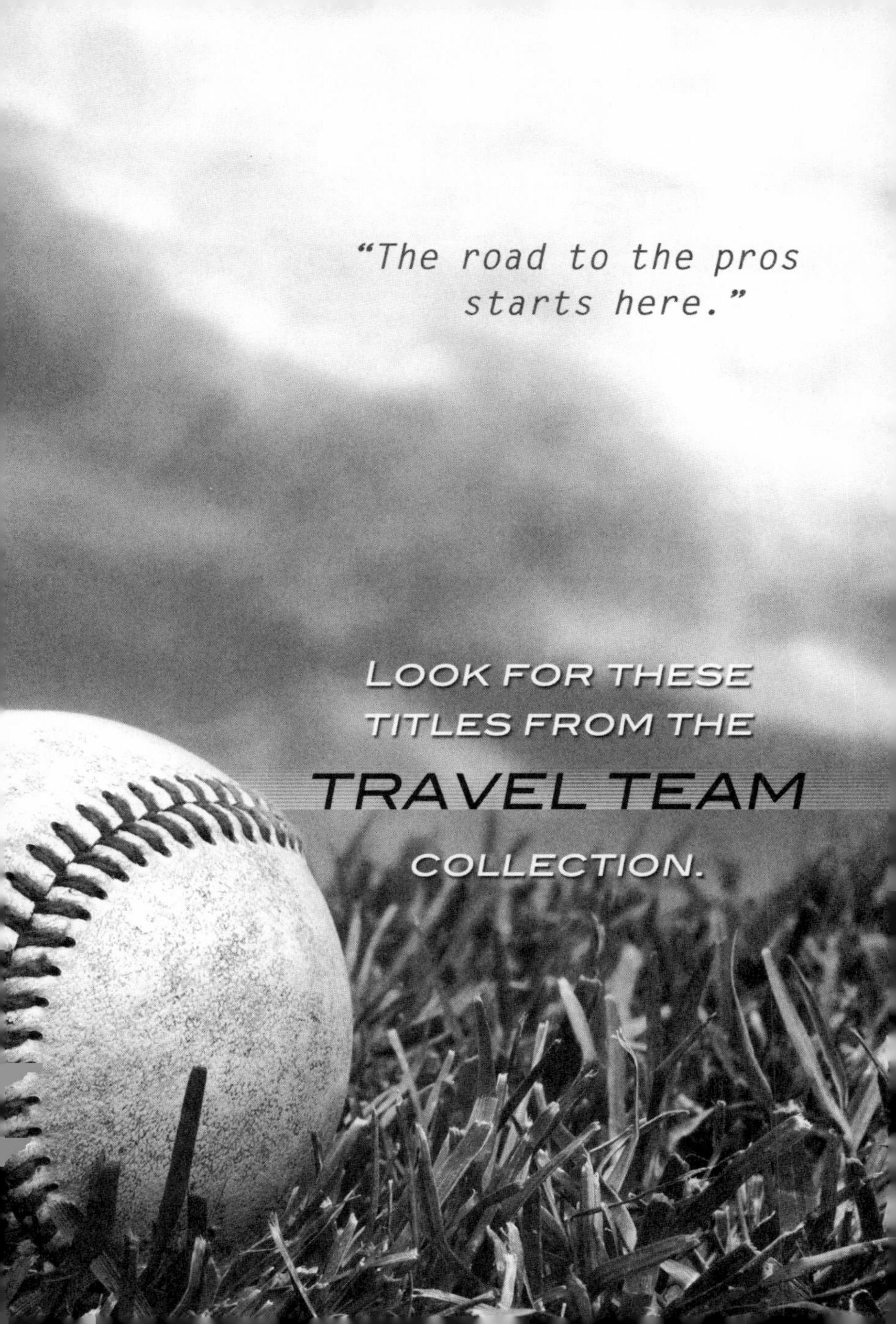
"The road to the pros
starts here."
LOOK FOR THESE
TITLES FROM THE
TRAVEL TEAM
COLLECTION.

THE CATCH

When Danny makes "the catch," everyone seems interested in him. Girls text him, kids ask for autographs, and his highlight play even makes it on SportsCenter's Top Plays. A sports-gear executive tempts Danny with a big-money offer, and he decides to take advantage of his newfound fame. Danny agrees to wear the company's gear when he plays. But as his bank account gets bigger, so does his ego. Will Danny be able to keep his head in the game?

POWER HITTER

Sammy Perez has to make it to the big leagues. After his teammate's career-ending injury, the Roadrunners decided to play in a wood bat tournament to protect their pitchers. And while Sammy used to be a hotheaded, hard-hitting, home-run machine, he's now stuck in the slump of his life. Sammy thinks the wood bats are causing the problem, but his dad suggests that maybe he's not strong enough. Is Sammy willing to break the law and sacrifice his health to get an edge by taking performance-enhancing drugs? Can Sammy break out of his slump in time to get noticed by major-league scouts?

FORCED OUT

Zack Waddell's baseball IQ makes him one of the Roadrunners' most important players. When a new kid, Dustin, immediately takes their starting catcher's spot, Zack is puzzled. Dustin doesn't have the skills to be a starter. So Zack offers to help him with his swing in Dustin's swanky personal batting cages.

Zack accidentally overhears a conversation and figures out why Dustin is starting—and why the team is suddenly able to afford an expensive trip to a New York tournament. Will Zack's baseball instincts transfer off the field? Will the Roadrunners be able to stay focused when their team chemistry faces its greatest challenge yet?

THE PROSPECT

Nick Cosimo eats, breathes, and lives baseball. He's a place-hitting catcher, with a cannon for an arm and a calculator for a brain. Thanks to his keen eye, Nick is able to pick apart his opponents, taking advantage of their weaknesses. His teammates and coaches rely on his good instincts between the white lines. But when Nick spots a scout in the stands, everything changes. Will Nick alter his game plan to impress the scout enough to get drafted? Or will Nick put the team before himself?

OUT OF CONTROL

Carlos "Trip" Costas is a fiery shortstop with many talents and passions. His father is Julio Costas—yes, *the* Julio Costas, the famous singer. Unfortunately, Julio is also famous for being loud, controlling, and sometimes violent with Trip. Julio dreams of seeing his son play in the majors, but that's not what Trip wants.

When Trip decides to take a break from baseball to focus on his own music, his father loses his temper. He threatens to stop donating money to the team. Will the Roadrunners survive losing their biggest financial backer and their star shortstop? Will Trip have the courage to follow his dreams and not his father's?

HIGH HEAT

Pitcher Seth Carter had Tommy John surgery on his elbow in hopes of being able to throw harder. Now his fastball cuts through batters like a 90 mph knife through butter. But one day, Seth's pitch gets away from him. The *clunk* of the ball on the batter's skull still haunts Seth in his sleep and on the field. His arm doesn't feel like part of his body anymore, and he goes from being the ace everybody wanted to the pitcher nobody trusts. With the biggest game of the year on the line, can Seth come through for the team?

SOUTHSIDE HIGH

ARE YOU A SURVIVOR?

check out all the books in the

collection.

BAD DEAL

Fish hates having to take ADHD meds. They help him concentrate but also make him feel weird. So when a cute girl needs a boost to study for tests, Fish offers her one of his pills. Soon more kids want pills, and Fish likes the profits. To keep from running out, Fish finds a doctor who sells phony prescriptions. But suddenly the doctor is arrested. Fish realizes he needs to tell the truth. But will that cost him his friends?

RECRUITED

Kadeem is a star quarterback for Southside High. He is thrilled when college scouts seek him out. One recruiter even introduces him to a college cheerleader and gives him money to have a good time. But then officials start to investigate illegal recruiting. Will Kadeem decide to help their investigation, even though it means the end of the good times? What will it do to his chances of playing in college?

BENITO RUNS

Benito's father had been in Iraq for over a year. When he returns, Benito's family life is not the same. Dad suffers from PTSD—post-traumatic stress disorder—and yells constantly. Benito can't handle seeing his dad so crazy, so he decides to run away. Will Benny find a new life? Or will he learn how to deal with his dad—through good times and bad?

Plan B

Lucy has her life planned: She'll graduate and join her boyfriend at college in Austin. She'll become a Spanish teacher, and of course they'll get married. So there's no reason to wait, right? They try to be careful, but Lucy gets pregnant. Lucy's plan is gone. How will she make the most difficult decision of her life?

Beaten

Keah's a cheerleader and Ty's a football star, so they seem like the perfect couple. But when they have their first fight, Ty is beginning to scare Keah with his anger. Then after losing a game, Ty goes ballistic and hits Keah repeatedly. Ty is arrested for assault, but Keah still secretly meets up with Ty. How can Keah be with someone she's afraid of? What's worse—flinching every time your boyfriend gets angry or being alone?

Shattered Star

Cassie is the best singer at Southside and dreams of being famous. She skips school to try out for a national talent competition. But her hopes sink when she sees the line. Then a talent agent shows up, and Cassie is flattered to hear she has "the look" he wants. Soon she is lying and missing rehearsal to meet with him. And he's asking her for more each time. How far will Cassie go for her shot at fame?